PENELOPE FRITTER: SUPER-SITTER

Book #1: The Chipster's Sister

BY JESSICA WOLLMAN
ILLUSTRATED BY CHRIS MACNEIL

Aladdin Paperbacks
New York London Toronto Sydney

ALADDIN PAPERBACKS

An imprint of Simon & Schuster Children's Publishing Division

1230 Avenue of the Americas, New York, NY 10020

Text copyright © 2005 by Jessica Wollman and Daniel Ehrenhaft

Illustrations copyright © 2005 by Chris MacNeil

All rights reserved, including the right of reproduction in whole or in part in any form.

ALADDIN PAPERBACKS and colophon are registered trademarks of Simon & Schuster, Inc.

Designed by Debra Sfetsios

The text of this book was set in Golden Cockerel.

Manufactured in the United States of America

First Aladdin Paperbacks edition June 2005

2 4 6 8 10 9 7 5 3 1

Library of Congress Control Number 2005920905

ISBN 1-4169-0089-6

For younger siblings everywhere

This is the story of Penelope Fritter.

It is also the story of suspense, mayhem, the triumph of good over evil (well, okay, technically the triumph of good over two very awful brats and a not-so-evil villain), shocking super powers, and three mysterious yet tasty smoothies.

PART I

Is There Anything He Can't Do?

CHAPTER ONE

The Invisible Girl

Penelope Fritter was invisible. And not invisible in the cool, magic-cloak, blockbuster-movie kind of way. She was invisible in the worst possible way. She was invisible in the symbolic way. People could *see* her. They just didn't *notice* her.

This was especially true at school.

Penelope went to Clearwater Elementary, where she was in the seventh grade. Unfortunately she might as well have not gone to school at all. It wasn't that people didn't like her, because Penelope was perfectly nice. She was really smart, too. She always got straight As and didn't even have to study all that hard. Only that didn't really help her in the popularity department.

The problem was that there was nothing about Penelope that made her stand out in a crowd. She wasn't loud or silly or great at kickball or an expert at blowing bubbles with bubble gum. She was just . . . Penelope.

Nobody ever saved her a seat at lunch. Nobody ever hung out with her at recess. Nobody ever talked to her in the hallway between classes.

Actually, that's not true. Last week somebody said, "Hi, my name is Fred. Are you a new student here?"

Penelope sighed. She had been going to Clearwater Elementary since kindergarten. She'd been in Fred's homeroom class for the past six years.

"I've been in your homeroom class for the past six years," she told Fred. "And last week I helped you with your math homework. My name is Penelope."

He laughed and said, "I don't think so. I know *everyone* in homeroom. But it's nice to meet you anyway, Priscilla." Then he walked off.

Even Penelope's teachers had a hard time remembering who she was. Just that afternoon her English teacher, Mr. Willard, forgot all about her.

"I have a paper here written by someone named . . .

Penelope," Mr. Willard said, grumbling. He wrinkled his bushy eyebrows and frowned at the class. "Hmm. Doesn't ring a bell. It's a shame too because this paper is really terrific. An A+ job. Whoever this Penelope is, she sure can write. Does anybody know her?"

"That's me," Penelope said.

Everyone turned to look at her.

"Penelope Fritter," she added.

Everyone's eyes widened, including Mr. Willard's.

"Fritter!" Mr. Willard exclaimed. "As in . . . *Chip* Fritter?"

"Yes, as in Chip Fritter," she said quietly. "But also as in Penelope."

CHAPTER TWO

The Exact Opposite of Invisible

Chip Fritter was Penelope's older brother. He'd graduated from Clearwater Elementary the year before. He was now in the ninth grade at Clearwater High.

And he was also the *exact opposite* of invisible.

Chip Fritter was *ultra* visible. He was *hyper* visible. People didn't just see him. People didn't just notice him. People *flipped out* over him. Parents, teachers, kids—it didn't matter. Here's an example: When Chip caught the flu last year, the entire school closed out of despair and the principal himself sent him a pot of

5

homemade chicken soup (true story). Everybody loved Chip. *EVERYBODY.*

Penelope loved Chip too, of course. He was her older brother, after all.

She just didn't understand what the big deal was.

CHAPTER THREE

What the Big Deal Was

"I can't believe you're Chip Fritter's sister!" Mr. Willard cried. "Why didn't you say something?"

Penelope shrugged. She wasn't sure what she was supposed to have said.

"Of course your paper is excellent!" Mr. Willard continued. "Chip must have helped you with it."

"Actually, I wrote it all by myself," explained Penelope.

"Of course, of course. Silly me," Mr. Willard stammered. He shoved Penelope's A+ paper toward her and moved on. "Chip was probably too busy—what with his

7

soccer games and amazing popularity. Why, that boy's a real superstar!"

"That's what they tell me," Penelope replied.

It was true. People told Penelope that Chip was "a real superstar" all the time. They also said stuff like "Chip Fritter is a true hero" and "Let's win one for the Chipster."

But mostly people asked, "Is there anything Chip Fritter can't do?"

I wish I had a penny for every time people asked me that question, Penelope liked to say to herself.

A long time ago she decided to put the pennies she wished for in an imaginary piggy bank. That imaginary piggy bank now held $716.82 in imaginary pennies.

In fact the very next question Mr. Willard asked was, "Is there anything Chip Fritter can't do?"

Penelope shrugged again. *Make that $716.83*, she thought.

Penelope personally thought the size of her imaginary piggy bank was a much bigger deal than what her brother could or could not do. But there wasn't much point in bringing that up. Nobody would have paid much attention anyway.

CHAPTER FOUR

A Big, Exciting Surprise

When Penelope came home from school that afternoon, her mother told her that she had a big, exciting surprise waiting! It was something truly amazing and incredible!

"What is it?" Penelope asked.

"Today Chip got picked to be president of his class!" Mom exclaimed.

Penelope tried to smile, but she couldn't quite manage. "Um . . . that's the big surprise?"

Mom laughed. "No, silly!" she said. "The surprise is that they didn't even have an election! Everybody

9

knew Chip was going to win. Everybody wanted to vote for him. So they just made him president! Just like that!"

"Oh," Penelope said. For some reason she didn't find the news all that surprising. She reached into her knapsack and pulled out her English paper. "Look—Mr. Willard gave me another A+."

"Of course he did, sweetheart," said Penelope's mother, barely glancing at the paper. "He knows how hard you worked. Anyway, we're all going out to Sips' Smoothie Saloon to celebrate Chip's victory."

That wasn't a big surprise either. Whenever the Fritter family had a reason to celebrate—meaning whenever Chip scored the winning goal in a soccer game, made yet another new friend, or rescued a hurt kitten from a treetop—the Fritter family piled into the car and headed to Sips' Smoothie Saloon.

Penelope wasn't exactly sure how many times they'd gone to Sips' Smoothie Saloon to celebrate Chip. But she figured the number was probably close to the number of imaginary pennies she had in her imaginary piggy bank.

"So how was your day, honey?" Mom asked.

Penelope opened her mouth to repeat the part about her A+ paper. But before she could say anything,

Chip came barreling through the front door.

"Chip!" Mom exclaimed. "We were just talking about you!"

"That's so funny!" Chip said. "I was just *thinking* about me!"

CHAPTER FIVE

Truly Tasty Dessert in a Cup

For the next hour, Chip told Penelope and Mom the story of his amazing, incredible, exciting day.

Then Dad got home from work, so Chip told the story again.

After that they all piled into the car and headed to Sips' Smoothie Saloon.

Sips' Smoothie Saloon was the most famous smoothie restaurant in all of Clearwater. It was named for its two owners, Seymour and Gwendolyn Sip. Nobody made a smoothie quite like the Sips. Nobody.

There was actually another smoothie guy in town, Vlad Black. He ran Vlad Black's Smoothie Stand. But his smoothies weren't nearly as good.

As to exactly what made the Sips' smoothies so good ... well, that was anyone's guess. The special homemade recipe was top secret. Legend had it that Seymour Sip received the recipe from super-intelligent aliens who felt that we poor human beings had suffered long enough without a truly tasty dessert in a cup.

Penelope didn't know if the legend was true. One thing was for sure, though: The Sips certainly knew how to make a delicious smoothie. *Way* better than Vlad Black's. In fact Penelope's mouth was watering during the entire drive to the restaurant. She knew exactly what flavor smoothie she wanted too. Strawberry. Penelope loved strawberry.

Unfortunately she forgot all about her delicious strawberry dessert in a cup the moment she walked through the door.

CHAPTER SIX

Why Penelope Forgot About Her Smoothie

The Sips had two children—two very awful brats named Will and Enid. Usually, Will and Enid stayed behind the counter with their parents.

But not tonight.

Tonight, for some reason, the children were "helping the customers." At least that was how Mr. and Mrs. Sip put it. Penelope had a hard time figuring out exactly how Enid and Will were helping, though. Enid was throwing huge globs of smoothie mix at everyone. Will was punching the smoothie-soaked people as they tried to flee the restaurant, shouting, "I LIKE PUNCHING PEOPLE!"

Neither Mr. Sip nor Mrs. Sip seemed to notice.

"Chip Fritter!" they both exclaimed from behind the counter. "What brings *you* here?"

"I was elected class president!" Chip exclaimed.

"He wasn't *elected*," Mom corrected. "They just *made* him president."

"The class elected not to have elections," Dad added proudly.

Mr. and Mrs. Sip smiled at each other. Then they smiled at Chip.

"Is there anything Chip Fritter can't do?" they both asked at the same time.

CHAPTER SEVEN

The First Annual Smoothie Convention

"So the Chipster was picked to be class president!" Mr. Sip cried. "Well done!"

"Sounds like our Chip deserves a smoothie on the house!" Mrs. Sip proclaimed.

She immediately began to mix up a special, jumbo-size, triple fudge brownie smoothie. Everyone smiled at Chip. (Well, everyone except Penelope.)

Will and Enid ran over to Chip and grabbed his hands.

"Will you play with us?" they shrieked. "Will you play with us? Will you?"

As you know, Penelope usually didn't enjoy being invisible. But at that moment she couldn't have been happier. Will and Enid were paying so much attention to Chip that they didn't notice her at all. Which meant, of course, that they weren't throwing smoothie mix at her or punching her.

"Look at how Will and Enid love Chip!" Mrs. Sip crooned. She handed Chip his free, special, jumbo-size, triple fudge brownie smoothie. Chip had to let go of Enid and Will because he needed both hands to lift it. The smoothie was *that* huge.

"Our little angels are usually so shy!" Mrs. Sip said.

"Well, it's no surprise they aren't shy with Chip," said Dad. "Chip is wonderful with kids."

"He sure is," Mom agreed.

Penelope rolled her eyes.

Mr. Sip stroked his chin. "I have a terrific idea," he said. "Why doesn't Chip come over and baby-sit Will and Enid tomorrow night? Vlad Black is hosting the First Annual Smoothie Convention, and Gwendolyn and I *must* attend. It would be so much easier for us if we could leave them at home. You know, in the hands of somebody who's so wonderful with kids."

Mom and Dad beamed at each other.

Mr. and Mrs. Sip beamed at each other too.

So did Will and Enid.

After that everyone beamed at Chip. (Well, everyone except Penelope.)

"Well, Chip?" Mom asked. "What do you say?"

"Gee, I'd love to baby-sit Will and Enid," Chip said, sipping from his special, jumbo-size, triple fudge brownie smoothie. "After all, kids—like most people—really do love me. The problem is, I have a soccer game tomorrow night, and I can't miss it. My team needs me."

"Of course they do," Dad agreed solemnly. "You're the captain."

Mr. Sip's face fell. "Oh . . . well, I understand," he said.

"I do too," Mrs. Sip said, sighing. But she sounded very disappointed.

"Um, could I have a strawberry smoothie please?" Penelope asked.

Nobody seemed to hear her.

Will and Enid blinked several times. Their lips began to twitch. Their eyes watered. "Does . . . does . . . does that mean Chip can't baby-sit us?" they asked, sniffling.

"I'm afraid so," Mr. Sip said gravely.

Both kids burst into tears.

Mrs. Sip dashed out from behind the counter and swept her children into a tight embrace. "There, there," she murmured. "I'm sure we'll figure something out."

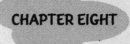

CHAPTER EIGHT

Penelope's Dad Has the Very Worst Idea in the Whole World

Right at that moment, Penelope caught Dad staring at her.

Uh-oh, she thought to herself.

"I have an idea," Dad said. "Why doesn't Penelope baby-sit for them?"

Mrs. Sip looked up from her sobbing children and frowned. "Who?"

"Penelope," Dad said, pointing to Penelope. "Chip's sister."

Every member of the Sip family turned to look at Penelope.

Judging from their blank expressions, you'd think that they'd never seen her before—even though she'd been to Sips' Smoothie Saloon almost as many times as she'd put imaginary pennies in her imaginary piggy bank.

"Chip has a sister?" Mr. Sip asked.

"Why, yes," Mom said. She pointed at Penelope too. "She's right here."

Penelope started shaking her head. "I don't think this is a very good idea," she said. "Baby-sitting, I mean."

Mrs. Sip smiled. "It's so nice to meet you, dear," she said. "Prudence, is it?"

"I don't have any experience baby-sitting," Penelope insisted.

"So, it's settled then," Dad announced. "Penelope will baby-sit the Sip children."

"I don't *want* to baby-sit the Sip children," Penelope said. "All I really want is a strawberry smoothie."

"Oh, you must be a wonderful athlete just like your brother. And I'm sure you have loads of friends just like Chip here," Mrs. Sip said, and smiled.

"Um, well, I don't really like sports," said Penelope. Mrs. Sip's smile faded. Now she just looked confused. "But, uh, I have been on the honor roll ever since I started school."

"Well, Patricia, if you're half as responsible as the

Chipster, I'm sure you'll do a great job," Mr. Sip said.

Penelope hung her head.

She wanted to tell them that she *wouldn't* do a great job. She wanted to tell them that she wasn't half as responsible as Chip or even a quarter as responsible or even a millionth as responsible. She wanted to tell them that hiring her to baby-sit their two awful brats was the very worst idea in the whole world.

She also wanted to tell them that her name was *Penelope*.

But she didn't. Chances are that nobody would have paid much attention anyway.

PART II

Penelope Baby-Sits the Two Very Awful Brats

CHAPTER NINE

The Very Strange House

The next night Mom and Dad dropped off Penelope at the Sips' house on their way to Chip's soccer game.

"We'll give Chip a big cheer for you!" Mom said to Penelope.

"We'll tell Chip how sorry you are that you can't see the game!" Dad called as they pulled away from the curb. "I'm sure he knows how much you want to be there!"

The car disappeared down the street.

Penelope's shoulders sagged.

The night was dark and windy.

There were wispy clouds covering the moon.

In other words, it was definitely *not* the kind of night that you'd want to hang out in a strange house you'd never hung out in before. Especially if you knew that there were two very awful brats waiting inside—two very awful brats who probably wanted to throw smoothie mix at you or punch you.

It's just for three-and-a-half hours, Penelope thought, marching up to the doorbell. *Will and Enid will be asleep most of the time, and I'll be able to get all of my homework done. It's not a big deal at all actually.*

But even as she said these words to herself, she knew she didn't believe them.

Ding-dong.

A moment later Mrs. Sip opened the door. She was wearing pearls and an evening gown. She smiled curiously at Penelope.

"Yes?" she said. "Are you selling cookies?"

"Uh . . . no," Penelope said. "I'm Penelope."

"What a pretty name!" Mrs. Sip exclaimed. She paused, confused. "So . . . what exactly *are* you selling? Candy? Are you trying to raise money for school uniforms?"

"No," Penelope said as she took off her backpack and coat. "I'm not selling anything. I'm here to baby-sit your kids."

Mrs. Sip laughed. "Oh, there must be some mistake! Chip Fritter's sister is supposed to baby-sit our kids!"

Penelope rolled her eyes. "I know," she said. "I *am* Chip Fritter's sister."

"You *are?*" Mrs. Sip cried. She laughed again. "Well, why didn't you say so? Come in, Peggy! Come in! How is Chip, by the way?"

CHAPTER TEN

Not Funny in a **Ha-Ha** Way

The inside of the Sips' house was sort of funny.

But it wasn't funny in a *ha-ha* way. It was funny in a weird and disturbing way.

For one thing, Penelope felt as if she were lost in a maze. She'd never been dragged around so many twists and turns in her life. And everywhere, all over the place, were framed photos of people drinking smoothies: big smoothies, small smoothies, strawberry smoothies, smoothies with whipped cream and double fudge and cherries on top.

29

Soon she felt dizzy.

"Will and Enid were here just a second ago," Mrs. Sip told Penelope. "I just saw the little cuties—"

"BOO!" two high-pitched voices screamed.

Penelope nearly jumped out of her skin.

Will and Enid poked their heads out from around the corner. They both burst out laughing: "MU-HU-HA-HA-HA!" It was the kind of loud, cackling laugh you hear sometimes in really scary movies.

"There the little angels are," Mrs. Sip crooned. "Will, Enid, you remember Persephone, don't you?"

Neither Will nor Enid said a word.

"Chip Fritter's sister?" Mrs. Sip said.

Will made an angry face. "Hey, how come Chip can't baby-sit us?" he asked.

"Yeah," Enid whined. "We love Chip. Chip's a real superstar."

"Well, Chip has an extremely important soccer game, sweeties," Mrs. Sip said. She looked down at her watch and gasped. "My goodness. It's nearly six forty-five! We're late for Vlad Black's smoothie convention!" She cupped her hands around her mouth and cried: "SEY-MOOOUR!"

"Coming!" Mr. Sip answered, bounding down the stairs.

Mr. Sip smiled when he saw Penelope. He was wearing

a tuxedo. His bow tie was crooked. So was his smile.

"Oh, I'm so glad you're here," he said, sounding relieved. "I'd like ten boxes of those caramel-coated Girl Scout cookies. And how about six boxes of the peanut butter?"

Penelope rolled her eyes.

"This isn't a Girl Scout, Seymour," Mrs. Sip said. "This is Chip Fritter's sister. She's here to baby-sit Will and Enid. Remember?"

"Oh, right!" Mr. Sip exclaimed. He slapped his forehead with his palm. "Chip Fritter's sister! How could I forget? How is the Chipster, by the way?"

Mrs. Sip grabbed her purse. "I think we'd better get going, Seymour."

"Right, right, of course," Mr. Sip agreed. He smiled again at Penelope. "Well, Pauline . . . it *is* Pauline, right? I thought so. We left a note on the refrigerator door with instructions. If there are any problems, we left our cell phone number, too. We shouldn't be home any later than ten o'clock. Okay?"

Before Penelope could answer, Mr. and Mrs. Sip scurried toward the door and slammed it behind them. *Smack!*

Penelope swallowed.

She turned back to Will and Enid.

They were gone.

The house was perfectly silent.

"Will?" Penelope called. "Enid?"

Nobody answered.

At that moment, Penelope had a very funny feeling about what was going to happen next—and not funny in a *ha-ha* way.

CHAPTER ELEVEN

The Most Important Rule of All

It took Penelope almost five whole minutes to find the kitchen. All of the weird twists and turns kept getting her lost. And when she finally did find the kitchen, there was still no sign of Will or Enid.

There was, however, a note on the refrigerator door. It said:

Dear Polly,

Thanks so much for looking after Will and Enid!

It's really too bad Chip couldn't be here with you, but

his soccer team is counting on him. I'm sure you understand. Here are the instructions:

1. Make sure Will and Enid are in their pajamas by 7 P.M.

2. They are both allowed ONE chocolate smoothie after they are in their pajamas. NO MORE THAN ONE APIECE. The chocolate smoothies are in the fridge.

3. Will and Enid should be brushed up and in bed by 8 P.M. Please read them a story before they go to sleep. (Just so you know, when we read them a story, we usually change a character's name to "Chip." They love that! ☺

4. This is <u>THE MOST IMPORTANT RULE OF ALL:</u> Whatever happens, DO <u>NOT</u> GO DOWN TO THE BASEMENT!!! The basement is STRICTLY OFF-LIMITS!!!

5. Help yourself to a snack!

If there are any problems, please call at 917-555-4378. See you at 10 P.M.!

The Sips

CHAPTER TWELVE

Penelope Gets Showered in Chocolate

After reading the note, Penelope felt a little better. The instructions didn't sound so hard. If she could just get Will and Enid to bed, she'd even have time to do a little homework. It'd be easy. That is, of course, if she could find Will and Enid . . .

Smack!

Something hit the back of Penelope's head.

Something wet.

And cold.

And a little slimy.

35

And whatever it was, it was now mushed into Penelope's hair and starting to drip down her neck.

"BULL'S-EYE!" two high-pitched voices cried.

Penelope whirled around.

Will and Enid were standing at the kitchen door. Will was holding a big fat glob of chocolate smoothie in one hand. Drops of brown goo fell from his fingers to the floor. Enid was waving a slingshot over her head. It, too, was dripping with brown goo. Both were laughing hysterically: "MU-HU-HA-HA-HA!" Neither one was wearing pajamas.

"What did you two just do?" Penelope demanded, even though she could already guess the answer.

"Catch me if you can!" Will suddenly shrieked.

"Catch me if you can!" Enid shrieked along with him.

They turned and bolted.

Penelope stood there in the kitchen. Chocolate smoothie mix dripped down her neck and into her shirt. She didn't really feel like catching Will and Enid. To be honest, all she really wanted to do was go home and take a shower. But the instructions on the refrigerator specifically said that Will and Enid had to be in their pajamas by seven o'clock. It was nearly seven o'clock now.

So Penelope went looking for them. She tiptoed back

around the twists and turns. She crept past all the framed photos of people drinking smoothies. But she couldn't find Will and Enid anywhere.

She did find a clock, however—just as it struck seven o'clock: *Gong! Gong! Gong! Gong! Gong! Gong! Gong!*

Penelope tugged at her hair.

What do I do? she asked herself nervously. *They're supposed to be in their pajamas right now! They're supposed to be eating chocolate smoothies, not flinging them at me with a slingshot! What do I do?*

She had no idea.

When her hands fell back to her sides, they were covered with brown goo.

CHAPTER THIRTEEN

Mr. Fix-It Plumber and Miss Clog-a-lot

As Penelope stared at her goo-covered hands, she heard a noise. It was a low, deep noise. It was a rumble, really. And it was coming from right over her head.

All at once, it started to rain—*INSIDE*.

Penelope looked up. An enormous crack had spread across the ceiling. Drops of water were gushing from it, soaking Penelope from head to foot.

Even under the best of circumstances, Penelope wasn't a huge fan of bad weather. And these were hardly the best of circumstances.

On the plus side, the indoor rain washed a lot of the chocolate smoothie out of Penelope's hair. But that was a very small plus.

"Ugh!" Penelope yelled. She ran from the room. (Well, she sloshed, if you want to know the truth.)

Much to her surprise, she bumped straight into Will and Enid.

Her eyes narrowed.

Will and Enid had changed clothes. Unfortunately they hadn't changed into their pajamas. Instead, they were both wearing striped overalls and rubber boots. Will was sporting a blue workman's cap. Enid was holding a large, wet wrench.

"What's going on?" Penelope demanded.

"I'm Mr. Fix-It Plumber, ma'am," Will announced in a deep voice.

"And I'm his trusty assistant, Miss Clog-a-Lot," Enid said.

Penelope wasn't sure what to say.

"The good news, ma'am, is that I've fixed your bathtub," Will stated. "The bad news is that you've got major problems with your toilet. But don't worry. I won't charge you extra for the overtime."

Enid nodded gravely. "He's doing you a big favor, ma'am," she said. "It's pretty nasty up there. We'd better get back to work."

"Is this some kind of joke?" Penelope asked.

"No, it's a game," Will said, switching back to his normal voice. "Enid and I play it all the time. We call it Mr. Fix-It Plumber and Miss Clog-a-Lot. You can play too, if you want."

"Yeah, it's just make-believe!" Enid said brightly. "If you want, you can be Miss Toilet Brush!"

They turned and disappeared down the hall.

Penelope glanced behind her. Rain was still pouring from the ceiling. The water was now ankle deep.

There was nothing make-believe about *That*.

So Penelope turned to chase after Will and Enid again.

But she stopped after only a few steps. Something blocked her path—something floating in the water at her feet.

It was a framed photo. Penelope figured it must have fallen off the wall during all the commotion.

The thing was . . . it wasn't just *any* framed photo.

It was a framed photo of Chip.

He was drinking a smoothie.

And he was smiling right at her.

CHAPTER FOURTEEN

The Straw That Broke the Camel's Back

Have you ever heard the expression "the straw that broke the camel's back"? Maybe you have. Maybe you've even wondered what it meant.

Well, at that moment, Penelope Fritter knew exactly what it meant. It meant the one teeny-weeny thing that suddenly made her *really, really mad.*

As to why it meant that, Penelope had no idea. There's probably some story behind that particular expression, but it doesn't matter very much—at least, not it in terms of this story.

Anyway, the straw that broke the camel's back for Penelope was seeing that picture of Chip floating at her feet. Seeing it made her mad at Will and Enid. It made her mad at Mr. and Mrs. Sip. It even made her mad at her parents. If Dad hadn't opened his big mouth and suggested that she baby-sit, she wouldn't be stuck in this weird and disturbing house with these two very awful brats in the first place.

Chip would be here.

And she'd be at home, peacefully doing her homework.

"WILL!" she shouted.

No answer.

"ENID!"

Still nothing.

"WILL AND ENID!" she screamed so loudly that her face turned bright red. "COME HERE RIGHT NOW!"

This time, she heard the sound of muffled giggles.

That's it, she said to herself. *I'm finding those two very awful brats and getting them into their pajamas if it's the very last thing I ever do!*

CHAPTER FIFTEEN

A Very Important Decision

The sound of the giggles seemed to be coming from the direction of the kitchen.

So Penelope dashed around the twists and turns. She ran past the framed photos of people drinking smoothies, splashing as she went.

But when she got to the kitchen, it was empty.

Penelope scowled.

She was breathing very hard from running and splashing. She looked one way, then another, then another—but all she saw was a growing flood. Her eyes wandered over to the note on the refrigerator door:

> *If there are any problems, please call at 917-555-4378. See you at 10 P.M.!*

Well, she couldn't find Will and Enid. *And* she was soaking wet. *And* the first floor was flooded. *And* she was very mad. *That* was certainly a problem.

Several problems, in fact.

She ran to the phone and punched in the number.

"Hello," a message answered. "This is Seymour Sip. I can't take your call right now. I'm on my way to Vlad Black's smoothie convention. So please leave—"

Penelope slammed the phone back down on the hook.

Okay, she thought. If the Sips couldn't help her, maybe Mom and Dad could. She quickly dialed Dad's cell phone number.

"Hello," a message answered. "This is Chip Fritter's dad. I can't take your call right now. I'm rooting for the Chipster at a big soccer game—"

Penelope hung up again.

And then she noticed something.

She was standing right next to the basement door.

There was a big sign on it. It said:

DO NOT ENTER!!! THIS MEANS <u>YOU</u>!!!

She noticed something else, too.

There was a noise coming from behind the door. A sort of *bump bump bump*. The sort of *bump bump bump* two very awful brats might make. Especially if those two very awful brats were trying to torture their baby-sitter by breaking the rules.

Penelope smiled to herself. *If Will and Enid can break the rules,* she thought, *then so can I.*

It was only fair, after all.

So Penelope decided to head down to the basement to look for Will and Enid.

PART III

The Forbidden Basement

CHAPTER SIXTEEN

Another Indoor Rainstorm

Penelope flicked on the light and tiptoed downstairs.

The wooden steps creaked under her feet. The *bump bump bump* grew louder the closer she got to the bottom.

"Will?" she whispered. "Enid?"

Nobody answered.

Her heart started to thump.

Maybe this isn't such a good idea, she thought. But . . .

When Penelope finally did get to the bottom, she frowned.

Will and Enid were nowhere to be seen.

Not only that, but the basement looked extremely boring.

Sure there was a humongous smoothie-making machine, just like the one the Sips had at their Smoothie Saloon. There was also a big refrigerator. And there were a bunch of pipes, too—the kind of pipes you'd see in any old basement.

But that was pretty much it. It wasn't like there was a bunch of super-intelligent aliens hiding out down here or anything.

Penelope shook her head. *What's the big deal about this place?* she wondered. *Why is it strictly off-limits?*

Just then, one of the pipes started to shake.

As it shook, it made a loud noise. *Bump bump bump.*

A-ha! Penelope thought. So *that's* where the noise was coming from. Will and Enid had nothing to do with it. On the other hand, she supposed their game of Mr. Fix-It Plumber and Miss Clog-a-Lot could have had something to do with it.

Bump bump bump!

The pipe was shaking pretty violently. It was almost … shimmying. Penelope took a step back. It looked like the pipe was about to explode.

Bump bump … KA-BOOM!

Sure enough, the pipe *did* explode. And the explosion

showered her in another indoor rainstorm.

Only . . . this particular indoor rainstorm was dirty.

And stinky.

And suspiciously brown.

On the plus side, it only lasted for two seconds. But that was a very small plus.

CHAPTER SEVENTEEN

Penelope Decides to Follow One Instruction

As Penelope stood there dripping with dirty, stinky, suspiciously brown water, she felt a lump growing in her throat. Tonight was quickly shaping up to be the very worst night of her entire life.

She'd been caught in two indoor rainstorms.

She hadn't been able to get Will and Enid into their pajamas.

She hadn't even been able to *find* Will and Enid.

Come to think of it, she hadn't followed *any* of the

Sips' instructions, not even helping herself to a snack.

What am I going to do? Penelope wondered miserably. The Sips' house was flooded. A picture of Chip was floating around upstairs somewhere. Will and Enid were still on the loose. And they probably weren't even wearing their pajamas.

Worse, Mr. and Mrs. Sip seemed to believe that Will and Enid were "little angels." So Penelope would probably get blamed for the disaster. After all, she'd ventured into the forbidden basement. She'd broken the most important rule of all.

For all she knew, the Sips might even make *her* pay to repair their house. And she couldn't. She didn't have any money of her own except the imaginary pennies in her imaginary piggy bank. Plus the Sips were only paying her a dollar an hour to baby-sit. At that rate, she would never make enough money to pay for *any* repairs. Not unless she baby-sat Will and Enid every night for the next hundred years. But by then she'd be an old woman, and Will and Enid would have long since destroyed the house. Actually, judging from the way things were going tonight, Will and Enid would have long since destroyed the whole *town.* Maybe even the entire *planet.*

Penelope sniffed. She wiped her eyes.

What am I going to do? she asked herself for what seemed like the millionth time.

She had no idea. But all this worrying was making her hungry.

At the very least, she figured she could follow one instruction: She could help herself to a snack. It wasn't much. But it was a start.

CHAPTER EIGHTEEN

The Three Tasty Yet Mysterious Smoothies

Penelope walked over to the big refrigerator and opened it.

Her eyes narrowed.

Inside the refrigerator were three large vats, sitting in an open box. The box had a sign on it. The sign said:

Preliminary Experimental Smoothie Test Formulas

DO NOT OPEN! THIS MEANS YOU!!!

Well, Penelope figured she had already broken one rule tonight. So there wasn't much point in paying any attention to this rule. Besides, grown-ups usually made a big deal out of nothing. Like Chip's soccer game.

The first vat was marked P.E.S.T. Formula #0011: Mellow Marshmallow.

Penelope unscrewed the cap and dipped her finger into the mix.

Yum, she thought. It tasted just like hot roasted marshmallows, which was pretty amazing, considering the smoothie mix was ice cold.

The second vat was marked P.E.S.T. Formula #0012: Whole Lotta Hazelnut.

Penelope gave that one a try too. It was even yummier than the first. It tasted exactly the way her parents' coffee smelled in the morning—but extra sweet.

The third vat was marked P.E.S.T. Formula #0013: Superpower Strawberry.

This vat also had a little warning written under its label. The warning said:

WARNING!!!

CREATED BY SUPER-INTELLIGENT ALIENS!!!

SIDE EFFECTS MIGHT INCLUDE THE APPEARANCE OF SHOCKING SUPERPOWERS!

DO NOT EAT UNLESS YOU HAVE AN HOUR TO SPARE!

Penelope's jaw dropped.

"Wow," she said out loud.

Normally, she didn't talk out loud to herself. But just imagine how YOU would feel if you found out that a crazy legend you'd heard your entire life was TRUE.

The Sips' homemade smoothies really were created by super-intelligent aliens. Or one of the desserts in a cup was, anyway.

No wonder the Sips didn't want anyone coming down here. They had a huge secret to hide. They were probably worried that someone would find out. They might even be worried that someone would try to steal the secret recipe.

Of course. It all made perfect sense now. Well, almost.

As Penelope stood there and stared at the vat, her mouth started watering. She *loved* strawberry.

The way she figured it, she'd already tried the other two flavors. So she might as well try this one, too.

And the truth was, she could use some shocking superpowers. They would probably come in handy for cleaning the house and getting Will and Enid to bed.

Besides the Sips wouldn't be home until ten. The clock on the basement wall said seven fifteen. She had more than an hour to spare. She had more than two hours to spare.

So Penelope dipped her finger in the P.E.S.T. Formula #0013.

It was even yummier than the other two combined.

CHAPTER NINETEEN

That Feeling You Get When You Eat Too Much Food

Penelope couldn't stop at just one bite. P.E.S.T. Formula # 0013 was just too good.

So Penelope dipped her finger into the vat again.

And again.

And again.

Pretty soon Penelope started using her whole hand. Then both hands. She must have been hungrier than she thought. She kept shoveling huge globs of pink smoothie into her mouth, one huge glob after another.

In less than a minute, Penelope emptied the entire vat.

She took a deep breath.

Uh-oh, she thought.

You know that feeling you get when you eat too much food? That feeling like somebody's blowing up a balloon in your stomach? And you really want them to stop, because there isn't enough room in your stomach for a balloon? But they won't stop, and the balloon just keeps getting bigger and bigger?

Well, that's how Penelope felt. She clutched at her stomach and groaned. She probably shouldn't have eaten so much so fast. But she couldn't help herself.

"Oof," she grunted.

Grunting made her feel a little better. But not much.

I need to sit down for a second, she decided.

Penelope turned the empty smoothie vat over so she wouldn't have to sit on the wet basement floor.

And that's when she saw it.

Taped to the bottom of the empty vat was another note. This one read: SUPER SECRET INGREDIENTS TO P.E.S.T. FORMULA #0013.

Ordinarily Penelope never read food ingredients. It

was fun to *eat* food, not read about it. Besides, who cared how much flour, eggs, and sugar were used to make, say, an Oreo?

But the ingredients for P.E.S.T. Formula #0013 were different. Each ingredient was written in a word scramble. The only way for Penelope to truly find out what was in the huge vat of strawberry smoothie she'd gobbled up was to unscramble each and every word.

And Penelope loved word scrambles almost as much as she loved strawberries. She was great at them too.

Penelope grabbed a pen that was hanging from the refrigerator and sloshed over to the basement steps. Then she plopped down and got to work.

CHAPTER TWENTY

You Are What You Eat

The good news was that the word scramble was really easy. Penelope finished the whole thing in about five minutes.

The bad news was that once it was done, Penelope finally learned what the Sips used to make the delicious vat of strawberry smoothies. And, as is turns out, their ingredients were not very delicious at all. In fact they were pretty disgusting.

Here's a list of the super secret ingredients:

P.E.S.T. FORMULA #0013—SUPER POWER STRAWBERRY (*WARNING: Do not read on a full stomach—especially one that's full of P.E.S.T. FORMULA #0013*)

(If you'd like to unscramble the ingredients yourself, go right ahead. Penelope's answers are at the bottom of this page.)

ILKM

RAGSU

LINEA NOTS*

FRUFNADD FLEAKS

ACT TIPS

SHAMED STRAW

WERRIESBRATS

*GACIMAL ITIGEDRENN

Penelope felt even worse than before. It's one thing to pig out, but pigging out on alien snot, dandruff flakes, cat spit, and mashed warts is another thing entirely.

"Ugh," she moaned, clutching at her stomach. She wondered if the Sips used the same ingredients to make all of their smoothies—minus the magical alien snot, of

MILK, SUGAR, *ALIEN SNOT, DANDRUFF FLAKES, CAT SPIT, MASHED WARTS, STRAWBERRIES
*MAGICAL INGREDIENT

course. After all P.E.S.T. Formula #0013 didn't really taste all *that* different from the strawberry Smoothie they served at the Smoothie Saloon.

This thought made Penelope moan even louder.

I've eaten hundreds of smoothies over the years. It's disgusting, Penelope thought to herself as she closed her eyes and rubbed her too full belly.

And then a funny thing began to happen. Penelope started to get very sleepy.

Sure, her stomach still hurt. And sure, she was a little worried she was going to be sick from eating all of that alien snot. Then, of course, there was the flooded house to deal with, along with finding Will and Enid and changing them into their pajamas. It wasn't like Penelope *forgot* about the stuff she had to do.

But before she did anything, she had to take a nap. She was as sure of that as she was of the fact that the Sips put mashed warts into their delicious smoothies. Penelope was exhausted. She could barely even stand up.

So she leaned back on the steps and closed her eyes.

I'll just doze for a couple of minutes, she promised herself with a yawn. *And then I'll go up and take care of everything I need to take care of.*

CHAPTER TWENTY-ONE

Items for Babies

When Penelope opened her eyes again, her stomach still hurt. But the strange thing was, it didn't hurt on the *inside* anymore. It hurt on the *outside*.

She glanced down.

Her eyes bulged.

"Whoa!" she cried.

As you know, Penelope didn't usually talk to herself out loud. But there was some kind of belt tied around her waist. It was big and thick and black. It was tied very tightly, which was why it hurt. And it had a lot of pouches. The pouches were packed with all sorts of weird items.

Penelope frowned. She took a closer look.

One of the pouches held a small bottle. The bottle was labeled SUPER STICKY BABY POWDER.

Another pouch held a clothespin. The clothespin was labeled SUPER CLOTHESPIN OF TRUTH.

And another pouch held a . . .

Wait a second, Penelope said to herself.

Was that a diaper dispenser? Yes. Yes, it was. It was labeled SUPER ABSORBENT DIAPERS.

There was also a diaper pin stuck into the pouch, labeled SUPER STRONG DIAPER PIN.

Suddenly it hit her.

All these items were for *babies.*

What on earth? she wondered. She actually felt a little insulted. She was not a baby. No. She was a baby-*sitter.* A very miserable baby-sitter, true. But still.

Penelope scowled and tugged at the belt. It wouldn't come off. No matter how hard she yanked and pulled and squirmed, it stayed put.

Finally she gave up.

That's when she noticed the very last pouch.

In it was a teeny-weeny little black book.

CHAPTER TWENTY-TWO

The Teeny-Weeny
Little Black Book

Penelope pulled the book out of its pouch and opened
to the first page.

*Congratulations! You have eaten our experimental
strawberry smoothie. We hope it was good. You now
have shocking superpowers that will last you the rest
of your life, thanks to the super items on your super
belt. We have tailor made these super items to fit
your every special need. Whenever you need to call*

upon your shocking superpowers, all you have to do is eat something strawberry. Remember: STRAW-BERRY = SUPERPOWERS!

And remember too that this is no small honor. Now that you have shocking superpowers, you have joined the ranks of other amazing superheroes across your humble little planet. That's right! Consider yourself the proud comrade of Bad Breath Billy, Ms. Leapfrog, Charlie Chores, and Round Round Robin, also known as Super Bouncy Girl and occasionally referred to as What's-Her-Face in some parts of the United States and Canada.

Penelope stopped reading.

She wasn't sure if she wanted to read any further.

For one thing, the part about the superpowers lasting the rest of her life made her a little nervous. Did that mean she would have to wear this belt for the rest of her life too? Not only was it uncomfortably tight, it was also . . . well, ugly.

For another thing, she didn't exactly feel honored to be joining the ranks of superheroes such as Bad Breath Billy and What's-Her-Face. To be honest, they didn't sound very amazing. They sounded sort of . . . well, dumb.

Plus, she was still pretty upset about eating all of those disgusting ingredients.

She turned the page.

Don't worry! You don't HAVE to become a superhero.

Penelope let out a big sigh of relief.

Should you choose to refuse this tremendous honor, all you have to do is

Splat!

Penelope blinked.

A big glob of dirty, stinky, suspiciously brown water had landed smack in the middle of the page. The ceiling was still leaky.

Uh-oh, Penelope thought.

The dirty, stinky, suspiciously brown water soaked the notebook paper and blurred the words. She squinted and strained and narrowed her eyes, but no matter how hard she tried, she couldn't read what came next. Not a single word. So she turned the page.

Congratulations! We are so happy you've decided to become a superhero! Here's the problem, though:

You've been asleep for nearly an hour, so your super-powers are about to run out. The super items' super-powers last for only an hour at a time. I'd get moving if I were you.
Sincerely,
The Super-Intelligent Aliens

Penelope gasped.

I've been asleep for nearly an hour? she asked herself in a panic.

She looked up at the clock on the basement wall.

Oh, no! Sure enough, it was nearly eight. Which meant that Will and Enid should be in bed. Which meant that they'd been running wild for the past forty-five minutes ... Penelope turned and started scrambling up the stairs.

"WILL!" she cried. "ENID!"

Neither one answered.

By the time Penelope reached the top step, she had a very bad feeling that this night was going to turn out even worse and weirder than it already had.

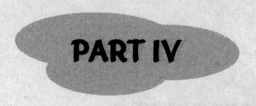

PART IV

Worse and Weirder

CHAPTER TWENTY-THREE

Penelope Learns That She, Will, and Enid Aren't Alone

Penelope burst back into the kitchen. Her plan was to run upstairs and put Will and Enid to bed as fast possible.

Unfortunately the plan didn't quite work out. On her way through the kitchen, she ran right smack into something.

"Oof!" Penelope cried.

She took a step back and scowled.

As it turns out, she didn't run into some*THING*.

She ran into some*ONE*.

Someone *BIG*.

A grown-up. A big burly man to be exact.

Uh-oh, Penelope thought to herself.

Whomever this big burly man was, he was dressed in black. He wore a black sweat suit. He also wore black sneakers, black gloves, and a black cap. A black handkerchief covered most of his face.

In other words, his entire body was covered in black—except for his big black eyes.

The big black eyes stared right at Penelope.

Penelope stared back at them.

And then she realized something.

The eyes didn't look evil, as you might expect they would. They didn't look mean or even scary. They looked frightened, probably even more frightened than Penelope's eyes looked.

Then the big burly man—whomever he was—started backing away from Penelope.

That's where he ran into trouble.

You see, the house was still flooded. The kitchen floor was soaked, so his sneakers began to slip. He began to lose his balance. His eyes widened. He waved his arms. His legs flew out from under him. . . .

"WHOA!" he yelled.

And with that, he landed with a *splat*—right on his back.

CHAPTER TWENTY-FOUR

A Big Surprise

Penelope winced. That *splat* looked sort of painful.

Of course, she wasn't terribly concerned about the big burly man. She was still pretty frightened of him.

So she turned to run back down to the basement.

But then *she* lost her balance on the soaking wet floor.

"WHOA!" she cried.

She skidded across the kitchen. And as she skidded, the teeny-weeny little black book on her belt kept poking into her belly.

Suddenly she remembered, *I have shocking super-powers!*

But then she thought, *Wait a second. If I have shocking superpowers, then why am I skidding across the floor? Why am I such a klutz?*

She didn't know the answers, but maybe the teeny-weeny black book could help.

So as soon as she stopped skidding, she pulled out the teeny-weeny black book and opened to page five.

Congratulations! You've just caught a burglar. If I were you, I'd tie up his hands and use your Super Strong Diaper Pin to hang him up on the laundry line. And remember, you don't have much time!

"Ow," the man mumbled from the floor.

Penelope shoved the teeny-weeny black book back into its pouch. So, she should probably tie up the man's hands. With what, though?

A-ha! she thought. She could use his black handkerchief!

She bent down beside him and snatched it off his face.

All at once, she gasped.

"Oh, my gosh!" she cried. "I know you!"

She most certainly did.

Because the big burly man lying on the flooded kitchen floor was none other than Vlad Black—the owner of Vlad Black's Smoothie Stand.

CHAPTER TWENTY-FIVE

An Even BIGGER Surprise

"What are *you* doing here?" Penelope asked. "I thought you were hosting a smoothie convention."

"Uh . . . I . . . I don't know what you're talking about, young lady," Vlad Black stammered. "I'm the Sips' house-keeper."

Penelope frowned. "No you're not," she said. "You're Vlad Black."

"No, I'm not Vlad Black," he replied. "It's funny. People . . . um, people mistake me for Vlad Black all the time. He's the guy who owns the smoothie stand, right? Boy, I really love his smoothies! I think they're the best in town. Much better than the ones at Sips' Smoothie Saloon."

Penelope's eyes narrowed. She didn't believe a word this big burly man was saying. He *was* Vlad Black. She was sure of it.

She had an idea about how she could prove it too.

Penelope yanked the Super Clothespin of Truth off her belt. And then she snapped it right on the big burly man's nose.

"Hey!" he cried.

(By the way, you might want to pinch your fingers over your nose as you read what the big burly man said next. That way, you'll sound exactly like him.)

"Now who are you?" Penelope demanded.

"Vlad Black," the big burly man admitted shamefully.

Penelope nodded. "I thought so," she said.

"It was all a trick," Vlad Black squeaked.

"What was all a trick?" Penelope asked. "What do you mean?"

"There is no smoothie convention," Vlad Black confessed. "I made the whole thing up so I could trick the Sips into leaving their house for a while. My devious plan was to come here to steal their secret homemade recipe while they were out. I wanted to figure out what makes their smoothies so much better than mine."

"Really?" Penelope asked.

"Really," he said, and groaned. "You have no idea what it's like for me. Everybody compliments the Sips' smoothies all the time. But nobody ever says a word about mine!"

Penelope sighed. She didn't know what to say. She actually felt sorry for Vlad Black. After all, his plan had failed. Worse, he'd ended up flat on his back on a flooded kitchen floor. Worse than that, he was right. The Sips' smoothies were much better than his.

But Penelope mostly felt sorry for him because she knew how he felt. After all, everybody complimented Chip all the time too. And nobody ever said a word about her. In fact most of the time they didn't even seem to notice her at all.

Penelope gulped. Maybe she should just give the ingredients to P.E.S.T. FORMULA #0013 to Vlad Black? He'd probably have a pretty hard time finding alien snot anyway.

CHAPTER TWENTY-SIX

The BIGGEST Surprise Yet

"So who are *you*?" Vlad Black asked Penelope.

"I'm Penelope Fritter," she said.

His forehead wrinkled. "Who?"

"The Sips' baby-sitter," she explained.

"The Sips' baby-sitter?" he cried. "But the Sips *never* hire a baby-sitter! They always take those two awful brats with them whenever they go out! That's why I planned it this way!"

"I know," Penelope said. "I'm sorry. But I guess since tonight was supposed to be a formal occasion—"

"Wait, did you say that your last name was Fritter?" Vlad Black interrupted. "As in . . . *Chip* Fritter?"

Penelope rolled her eyes. She didn't feel quite as sorry for Vlad Black as she had a second before.

Suddenly he squirmed and tried to make a run for it.

After that she felt even less sorry for him.

"Not so fast!" Penelope barked. She grabbed the back of Vlad Black's shirt. "You're staying put until the Sips get home! Understood?"

"Do I have to?" he asked.

"Yes, you have to," she stated. "It's not a choice." She tied up his hands with his black handkerchief. Then she dragged him by his shirt into the backyard.

Vlad Black kept trying to escape, but he couldn't. Every time he tried to run, his sneakers slipped on the grass. They were still soaking wet from the flooded kitchen floor.

"You're not going to call the police, are you?" he asked, his voice quaking.

Penelope shrugged. She pinned him to the clothesline with her Super Strong Diaper Pin. "I don't know," she said. "I haven't decided yet."

"Please don't," he begged. "I really hate getting in trouble."

"Well . . ." Penelope wondered whether she should call the police or not. Vlad Black did seem to understand that he'd done something wrong. And he hadn't gotten away with stealing anything. Plus he and Penelope did have similar sorts of problems. On the other hand, he did carry a photo of Penelope's problem around in his wallet. . . .

But before she could make up her mind, something happened that made her forget all about Vlad Black. (Well, almost anyway.)

Two very high-pitched voices screamed: "BOO!"

Penelope looked up.

There—swinging on the telephone wire high above the backyard—were Will and Enid. They both burst out giggling.

On the plus side, they had changed into their pajamas.

But given the fact that they were swinging from a telephone wire, that didn't even count as a plus. Not even a small one.

CHAPTER TWENTY-SEVEN

Penelope's Palms Begin to Sweat

"WILL!" Penelope shrieked, horrified. "ENID! Get *down* from there! It's *not safe!*"

Will and Enid giggled again.

"We can't get down!" Will yelled.

"Yeah!" Enid said. "We don't know how!"

"We only just figured out how to climb out here from our room!" Will added.

Penelope could hardly believe her eyes. Of all the dumb things she'd seen in her life, swinging from a telephone wire was by far the dumbest.

But there was no time to think about that. Penelope had to rescue them. Immediately. So she dashed back into the house. She splashed around the twists and turns and sprinted up to the second floor.

Luckily the second floor was perfectly dry. (So far anyway.)

It didn't take Penelope long to find Will and Enid's room. All she had to do was follow the sound of the giggles.

She ran to the open window.

Will and Enid were as happy as could be, swinging out there on the wire.

Penelope glanced down at Vlad Black, hanging on the clothesline far below. She swallowed. The telephone wire seemed much higher off the ground from up here than it did from down there.

"Will you come get us now please?" Will asked Penelope.

"Yeah," Enid said. She yawned. "I'm getting kind of bored."

"Um . . . okay," Penelope said, frowning.

The problem was, she wasn't a big fan of heights. In fact you might even say that she was *afraid* of heights. So she wasn't exactly thrilled with the prospect of climbing out on that wire to rescue Will and Enid.

"Come get us," Will whined.

"Yeah," Enid said. "Come get us."

Penelope's palms began to get sweaty. She was positive she would slip right off that wire the moment she tried to climb out on it. She was so afraid of heights that she forgot all about her shocking superpowers.

That is, until she caught a glimpse of the bottle of Super Sticky Baby Powder on her belt.

A-ha! she thought. *I can rub Super Sticky Baby Powder on my hands! That will keep me from slipping when I climb out on that wire!*

So that's what she did. She pulled out the Super Sticky Baby Powder and dumped it all over her hands— until they were as white as one of the Sips' vanilla smoothies.

CHAPTER TWENTY-EIGHT

Penelope Rescues the Two Very Awful Brats

Penelope leaned out the window and grabbed the telephone wire.

Hand over hand she climbed—first to Enid.

The thing was . . . the Super Sticky Baby Powder worked a little too well. She felt like she had glue on her hands. She couldn't slip even if she tried. It took all her strength just to yank her hands off the wire every time she moved.

On the plus side, she wasn't afraid of falling anymore.

"It's fun out here, isn't it?" Enid asked Penelope.

91

Penelope didn't answer. Instead, she just grabbed Enid.

Enid clung to Penelope's neck as Penelope climbed back to the bedroom window. It wasn't very pleasant. Penelope could hardly breathe.

Still, Penelope managed to dump Enid in her bed without any fuss.

Then Penelope climbed back across the wire, hand over hand, to Will.

Will clung to Penelope's legs as Penelope climbed back to the bedroom window. That was even less pleasant. Penelope's legs felt as if they were about to fall off. So she kicked—*hai-ya!*—and tossed Will right through the open window and into his bed.

CHAPTER TWENTY-NINE

Penelope Finally Says Good Night to the Two Very Awful Brats, Once and for All

"Read us a story, Patience!" Will shrieked.

"Yeah, Patsy!" Enid shrieked along with him. "Read us a story!"

Penelope closed the window and took a deep breath.

The very last thing she wanted to do was read Will and Enid a story. She wanted to tell them that they'd been very naughty. She wanted to make them help clean up the mess they'd made.

But she wasn't sure if they even knew the meaning of

the word *naughty.* Or the word *mess,* for that matter. She didn't know what to do.

That's when she decided to look at the teeny-weeny black book. It had helped her before after all. Maybe it could help her now, too.

Penelope pulled the book from its pouch and opened to page six.

Congratulations! You've gotten the two very awful brats into bed. Now read them this incredibly boring story to put them to sleep. It starts on the next page.

Penelope turned the page. "'This is the story of Penelope Fritter,'" she began to read.

"Who?" Will asked, yawning.

Penelope rolled her eyes.

"I like it when Mommy and Daddy change the main character's name to Chip," Enid said. She yawned too. "The stories are much better that way."

"Shh," Penelope whispered. Then she continued: "'It is also the story of suspense, mayhem, the triumph of good over evil . . .'"

By the time Penelope got to the word *evil,* Will and Enid were already snoring.

PART V

The Thrilling Conclusion

CHAPTER THIRTY

Penelope Makes a Mad Dash to Clean Up the Mess Before the Sips Get Home

Penelope shoved the teeny-weeny black book into its pouch and hurried downstairs.

She had lots of work to do and very little time to do it. After all, her shocking superpowers were only supposed to last an hour. And that hour was almost up.

She would definitely need shocking superpowers to clean up the mess on the first floor. The flood was still ankle deep.

Penelope stood at the bottom of the stairs, staring

down at her feet under the water. The situation didn't look good.

Then she noticed the Super Absorbent Diapers on her belt.

Hmm, she thought. *If those Super Absorbent Diapers are as shockingly powerful as the Super Strong Diaper Pin, the Super Clothespin of Truth, and the Super Sticky Baby Powder, then maybe the diapers can absorb all the water that's flooding the house!*

Using the diapers was certainly worth a try. Penelope didn't have any better ideas. So she started yanking Super Absorbent Diapers out of the dispenser. One right after another. Faster and faster. As she pulled them out, she tossed them into the water. Again and again and again.

Super Absorbent Diapers flew everywhere. *Whoosh!*

They landed in the water. *Splash!*

And you know what?

It worked!

The water level sank. It sank down past Penelope's ankles and down past the soles of her shoes . . . until the first floor was perfectly dry. (Well, except for the soggy diapers lying all over the place.)

Penelope laughed out loud. "Ha!"

Of course, she still had to clean up the forbidden basement.

So she ran downstairs. She yanked some more Super Absorbent Diapers from the dispenser and threw them into the water until all the water was gone. *Whoosh! Splash!* "Ha!"

Then—as fast as she could—she gathered up all the soggy Super Absorbent Diapers and tossed them into the big garbage can on the curb in front of the Sips' house.

She ran back inside.

She slammed the door behind her.

She was practically out of breath.

But she couldn't stop smiling.

She'd done it! The first floor was spotless! It was even cleaner than it had been before because all the water had given it a good wash!

Only . . . It wasn't *perfectly* spotless. Because lying there in the front hall, right in front of Penelope, was the framed picture of Chip that had fallen off the wall. And he was smiling right at her.

CHAPTER THIRTY-ONE

The Decision Not to Eat Strawberry

Amazingly enough, seeing that picture of Chip didn't bother Penelope one bit. It was no longer the straw that broke the camel's back.

Penelope picked up the picture and hung it back in its proper place on the wall.

And then she noticed something.

Her stomach didn't hurt anymore. It didn't hurt on the inside *or* the outside.

She looked down.

"Hey!" she cried out loud.

The belt was gone. It had simply disappeared. Just like that!

Then Penelope remembered: According to the teeny-weeny little black book, her shocking superpowers would last only an hour at a time. And that hour was definitely up.

She also remembered something else.

According to the teeny-weeny little black book, she had to eat something strawberry to get her shocking superpowers back.

Penelope stood there and thought for a moment.

She thought about how incredibly relieved she was that the house was clean and that the two very awful brats were in bed.

She thought about how this had been—without a doubt—one of the worst nights of her life.

She thought about how she never wanted to baby-sit *ever, ever* again.

If she never ever baby-sat again, she probably wouldn't have much need for any shocking superpowers. She wouldn't have to wear that tight, ugly belt. She wouldn't have to rescue any awful brats. And she wouldn't have to clean up flooded basements.

That settled it. The *last* thing Penelope ever wanted to do was to get her shocking superpowers back.

So she made a decision. *I'm never going to eat anything strawberry again,* she told herself.

And she meant it.

True, strawberry was her favorite flavor. True, the notion of never tasting anything so deliciously sweet as strawberry ever again was a little scary.

But it wasn't nearly as scary as the notion of having another night like the one she'd had tonight.

CHAPTER THIRTY-TWO

The Final Big Surprise

Suddenly the front door flew open. Mr. and Mrs. Sip marched into the house. Neither of them looked very happy. Or at least not as happy as they usually looked.

"Mr. and Mrs. Sip!" Penelope exclaimed. "You're home early!"

"I'm afraid so," Mr. Sip muttered. "Vlad Black canceled his smoothie convention. And he didn't even have the decency to tell us!"

Penelope tried to smile, but she couldn't quite manage. That was because Mr. Sip had just reminded her of something: Vlad Black was still hanging on the clothesline outside.

"Aw, look how sweet Pamela is!" Mrs. Sip crooned, pointing at Chip's picture. "She's admiring her brother's photo. We do that all the time too, dear. Chip's a real superstar."

Now Penelope had an even harder time trying to smile.

Mr. Sip walked right past her. He headed straight for the back door.

"Uh . . . where are you going?" Penelope asked him nervously.

"Why, just to see if the apron on the clothesline is dry," he said.

Penelope swallowed. If Mr. Sip went out to the clothesline, then he would see Vlad Black hanging on it with a clothespin pinched over his nose. And then Mr. Sip would ask Penelope how Vlad Black had gotten there. And then Penelope would have to admit that she'd broken the rules by eating all the P.E.S.T. Formula # 0013. . . .

But when Mr. Sip threw open the door, Penelope gasped.

Vlad Black was gone.

So was the Super Clothespin of Truth. So was the Super Strong Diaper Pin.

All that remained on the clothesline was Mr. Sip's apron.

CHAPTER THIRTY-THREE

The End

"What's the matter, dear?" Mrs. Sip asked Penelope. "You look pale."

Penelope shook her head. She was too shocked and baffled to answer.

All she could think was, *Vlad Black is gone! Where did he go? How did he escape from the Super Strong Diaper Pin? And what did he do with the Super Clothespin of Truth?*

Just as she finished asking herself these questions, there was a knock on the front door.

"Who is it?" Mrs. Sip called.

"It's Chip!" came the answer. "Chip Fritter!"

Mrs. and Mrs. Sip beamed at each other.

"Chip Fritter!" Mrs. Sip cried.

"The Chipster!" Mr. Sip cried.

"Come in, come in!" they both cried at the same time.

The door flew open. Chip ran into the house, wearing his muddy soccer clothes. Mom and Dad followed behind him. Both were holding banners.

"Guess what?" Chip said. "I won the soccer game!"

Mr. and Mrs. Sip beamed at each other again.

Mom and Dad beamed at each other too.

Then everyone beamed at Chip. (Well, everyone except Penelope.)

"Sounds like Chip deserves a smoothie on the house," Mrs. Sip said.

Penelope rolled her eyes.

"You know, I think Penelope deserves a smoothie too," Chip suddenly announced.

"Who?" Mr. Sip asked.

"My sister," Chip said, pointing at Penelope.

"Oh, right!" Mr. Sip cried. He slapped his forehead with his palm. "You have a sister! How could I forget?"

Penelope smiled at Chip. "You really think I deserve a smoothie?" she asked him. She couldn't believe it.

Chip patted her shoulder. "Of course you deserve a smoothie," he replied. "You had a really tough night. After all, you didn't get to see me score the winning goal."

The VERY End

Mrs. Sip leaned over and whispered something in Penelope's ear.

I bet you can guess what she said.

P.S.—Penelope Gets the Last Laugh

"So it's all settled," Mrs. Sip announced. "Two delicious smoothies for the Chipster and his sister coming right up!"

"You're both in for a real treat," Mr. sip added, grinning his crooked grin. "We've been experimenting with all kinds of new ingredients lately!"

Penelope thought for a minute. Then she cleared her throat and looked right at Chip.

"It's *so* nice of you to think of me," she said, smiling sweetly. "But I'd like you to have my smoothie. After all, you *really* deserve it."

"You know what," answered Chip with an understanding nod, "I think you're right!"

Everyone in the room laughed and cheered.

And, for the first time ever, Penelope joined them

THE END

QUESTIONS FOR NEXT TIME:

1. Will Penelope really be able to resist
eating strawberry?

2. Will she meet the other superheroes mentioned
in the teeny-weeny black book?

3. Will the Sips learn that Penelope ate all
their P.E.S.T. Formula #0013?

4. What happened to Vlad Black?

5. Will he try to steal the Sips' recipes again?

6. Will Chip ever stop being so full of himself?

7. How did super-intelligent aliens write a teeny-weeny instruction guide that predicted exactly what was going to happen in this story?

8. Who are these super-intelligent aliens, anyway?

For the answers to all these questions and more, please tune in to the next exciting installment of . . .

PENELOPE FRITTER, SUPER-SITTER!*

*Answers may not be included in the next installment.

Get a sneak peek at
Penelope Fritter's next superhero adventure!

MEET THE PHONEES

When we last left Penelope Fritter, Super-Sitter, she had just used her shocking superpowers to save the world and triumph over evil.

Well, okay . . . her superpowers weren't really all that shocking. And technically she never saved the world—just two very awful brats. Also, she hadn't exactly "triumphed," because the villain got away . . . and, to be honest, the villain—Vlad Black—wasn't so evil. He was just a crooked smoothie stand owner. And his smoothies weren't even that tasty.

But none of that is particularly important, because Penelope soon found herself embroiled in yet another amazing baby-sitting adventure—one packed with even MORE suspense and mayhem, not to mention frantic Jell-O eating, fiendish dessert pies, and freakish word scrambles. . . .

CHAPTER SEVEN

A Very Peculiar Family

Penelope didn't get very far.

In fact, she didn't get anywhere at all.

Four very tall grown-ups stood in the hallway just outside the gym, blocking her path—two tall men and two tall women. All four had gray hair.

At first, Penelope intended to run right past them. But then she began to stare.

As rude as she knew staring to be, she couldn't stop herself. There was just something very, well . . . *peculiar* about this bunch. One of the men was dressed just like Penelope's dad, in a suit. One of the women held a massively oversize handbag. And the other two grown-ups were dressed like children. The man wore striped shorts, a T-shirt, and a little cap with a plastic propeller on top. The woman wore pigtails and striped overalls, and she clutched a stuffed bear.

"Where are you going, dear?" the woman with the huge handbag asked. Her voice was surprisingly deep.

"Uh . . . me?" Penelope asked.

The woman threw her head back and laughed. The sound was loud and grating, like tires screeching on a wet road. "Yes, *you*!" she cried. "Don't you want to stay for Chip Fritter Fest?"

Penelope bit her lip. She wasn't sure if she wanted to answer that question.

"What's your name, dear?" the woman asked.

"Penelope."

"What a pretty name," the woman remarked. "Well, Penelope, we're new to town. We just moved here last week. It's sort of a funny story. We bought a lovely house. The previous owner abandoned it under mysterious circumstances." She tapped a long red-painted fingernail against her teeth. "Someone who might have gotten into trouble with the law . . . a crooked smoothie stand owner, if memory serves me correctly . . . I can't remember the name. . . ." Her voice trailed off. She arched an eyebrow.

"Vlad Black?" Penelope guessed.

The woman smiled. "Yes! Precisely! Do you know him?"

Penelope shifted on her feet. She gulped anxiously. She began to wish she *had* just run right past them. "Sort of," she admitted.

"Darling, you're making Penelope uncomfortable," the man in the suit quickly piped up. "We don't need to discuss Vlad Black." He stepped forward. "Allow us to introduce ourselves. We're the Phonee Family. P-H-O-N-E-E. My name is Mr. Phonee, and this is Mrs. Phonee. "And these are our darling children, Boris and Ophelia Phonee." He gestured toward the gray-haired man in the propeller cap and the gray-haired woman with the stuffed animal.

"Nice to meet you, Penelope," Boris said.

"Yes, very nice!" cried Ophelia. She laughed with the same terrible laugh as her mother.

Penelope tried not to wince.

"How old are you, Penelope?" Boris asked.

"Twelve," Penelope replied.

Boris's eyes lit up. "I'm nine!" he yelled. "I'll be twelve in three years!"

"I'll be twelve in five years, Penelope!" Ophelia added. "I'm seven!"

Penelope glanced between the two of them. She couldn't quite bring herself to believe that Boris was nine and Ophelia was seven. What seven-year-old had gray hair? But in spite of that, and in spite of the fact that this was most certainly the oddest family she had ever met in her life, Penelope couldn't help but smile— for a very simple reason.

All four Phonees had remembered her name.